To the loving memory of my grandmother, Elneatha Bryant, who was a strong influence in my life and encouraged me to attend church and commit my life to the Lord.

To the loving memory of my father, Bobby Bryant Sr., who was a strong and loving father.

To my wonderful mother, Mary, who helped me believe I could accomplish anything.

To my awesome sister, Eboni, whose personality brings joy to so many people around her.

To my Proverbs 31 wife, Cherita, the mother of our three amazing kids, whose passion, commitment, and dedication to our family are immeasurable.

www.mascotbooks.com

Trusting Timothy: A Story about Cheating

©2024 Bobby Bryant II, Bobby Bryant III, Ava Bryant, and Joseph Bryant. All Rights Reserved. No part of this publication may be reproduced, stored in a retrieval system or transmitted in any form by any means electronic, mechanical, or photocopying, recording or otherwise without the permission of the author.

Bible Scriptures are taken from the New King James Version and the New International Version.

For more information, please contact
Mascot Kids, an imprint of Amplify Publishing Group
620 Herndon Parkway #220
Herndon, VA 20170
info@mascotbooks.com

Library of Congress Control Number: 2024905432
CPSIA Code: PRKF0424A
ISBN-13: 978-1-63755-995-6

Printed in China

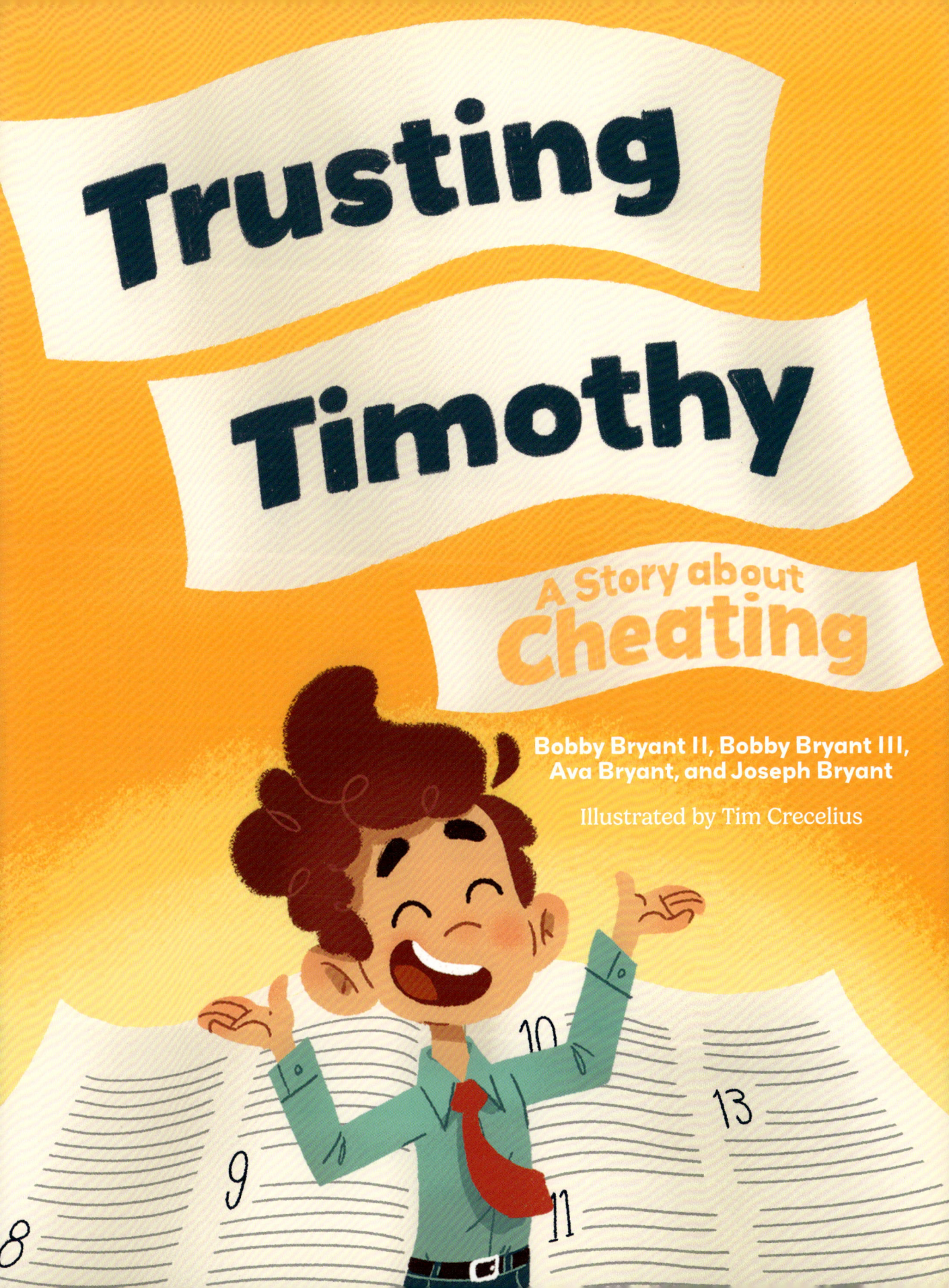

It was a beautiful sunny morning in late August, with the temperature in the midseventies. Timothy thought about his summer, which was an awesome, fun-filled one! He visited the Grand Canyon for the first time, and he attended a family reunion where he spent time with many family members he had not seen for a long while.

Timothy and his family had just moved into their new house, and he and his sister, Eve, would be starting a new school that day. Although Timothy had such a great summer and it was tough to see it come to an end, he was very excited to start at his new school and about the possibility of making new friends.

On the Sunday before school started, Timothy went with Grandma Lois to her church, which he always looked forward to. He enjoyed singing and clapping along with the choir, and he really loved Bible study. There were always some Bible verses that he would learn and try to memorize. His grandma would always tell him, "Continue to learn the Scriptures. God's Word will always help you in times of need, trouble, and in making tough decisions."

This past weekend, the verses Timothy learned were:

For nothing is secret that will not be revealed, nor anything hidden that will not be known and come to light.

LUKE 8:17 (New King James Version)

Whoever walks in integrity walks securely, but whoever takes crooked paths will be found out.

PROVERBS 10:9 (New International Version)

The integrity of the upright will guide them, but the perversity of the unfaithful will destroy them.

PROVERBS 11:3 (New King James Version)

Before Timothy knew it, the first two weeks of school had whizzed by. He was adjusting to his new school, and he really liked it.

He met some new friends named Johnny, Raymond, Charlie, and Curtis. Though he enjoyed spending time with them, he felt uncomfortable with some of the things they did.

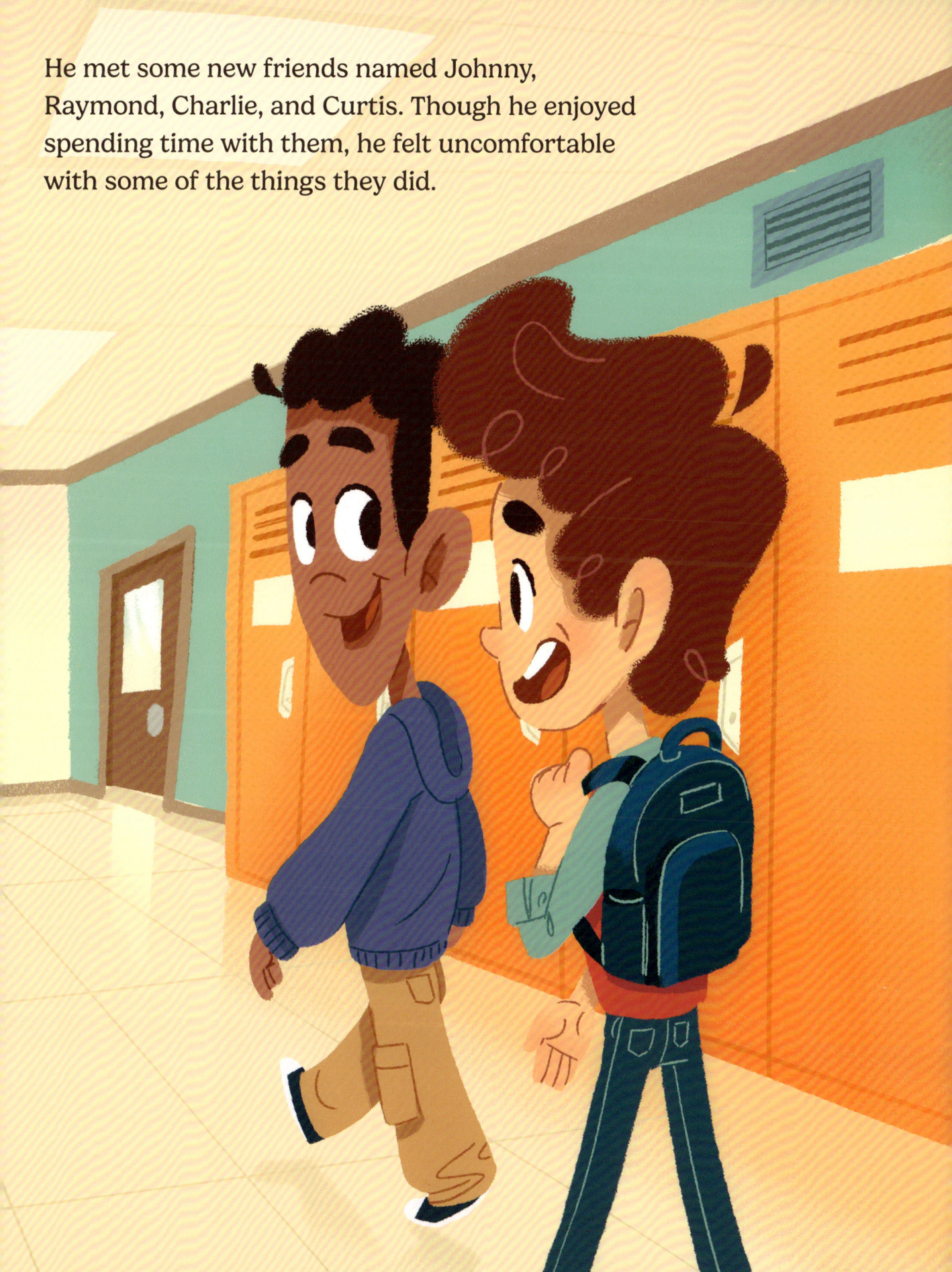

Monday of the third week of school was just beginning, and the morning bell rang through the halls. **RING!**

"Okay, settle down, class. Take your seats, and let's get started," said Mrs. Washington, the history teacher. "For tomorrow's class, we will have a test on the first four chapters of the book we read. It will be a multiple-choice test."

Many of the students quickly let out a groan of disapproval.

"Okay, okay. Take out your books, and we'll do a short review of the chapters," responded Mrs. Washington.

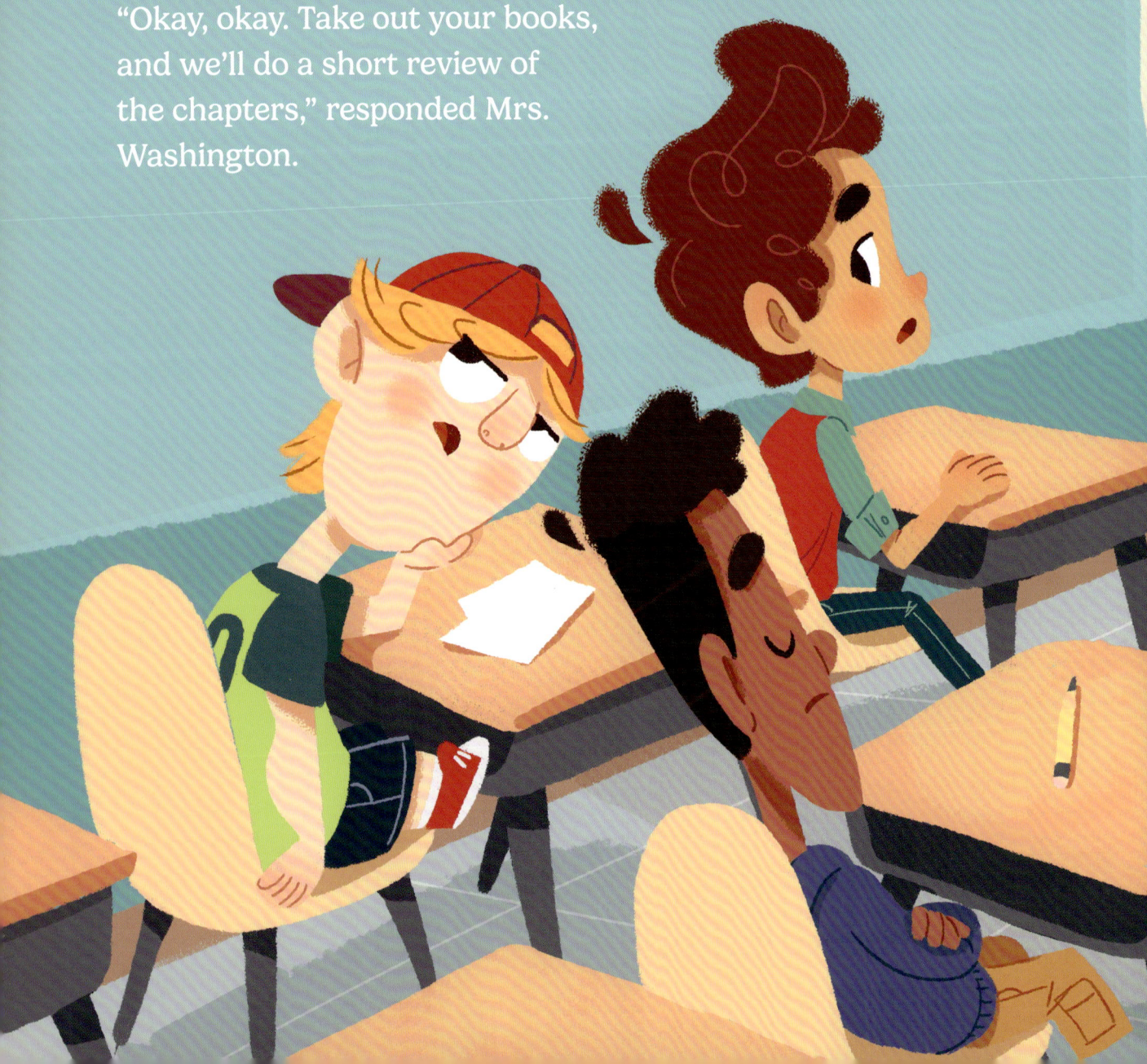

At lunchtime that day, Johnny said, "I hate taking tests! Why is Mrs. Washington giving us a test already?"

Raymond, Charlie, and Curtis agreed with him, but Timothy just listened to their conversation.

"But we don't have to worry about it," said Johnny. "Just before lunch, I looked through Mrs. Washington's desk for a copy of the test with the answers, and I found it! We can go over it after school today."

"Alright! Great job, Johnny!" said Raymond as he gave Johnny a high-five.

"Yes! Great job," repeated Charlie and Curtis.

Timothy sat there listening, feeling uncomfortable, until the end of lunch. He had a hard time focusing for the rest of the school day.

The final bell rang, and Johnny, Raymond, Charlie, and Curtis met up after school to go over the answers for the history test. Timothy decided not to meet them and went home instead. He didn't feel too good about the situation.

That night, Johnny tried calling Timothy to share the answers with him, but he didn't answer. Although the history test was probably going to be tough, and though it would be nice to have the answers, he remembered the verses he had memorized from Bible study from his last visit to Grandma Lois's church. Rather than returning Johnny's call, Timothy decided to spend the night studying for the history test.

The next morning, right before class began, Johnny asked, "Timothy, where were you after school yesterday? I also tried to call you last night to give you the answers."

"I just decided to study for the test," said Timothy.

"Why?" asked Johnny, as he, Raymond, Charlie, and Curtis looked at Timothy as if he were strange.

After history class ended, many of the students left with puzzled looks on their faces. Mrs. Washington's test was very challenging. Timothy was unsure of how well he did on the test, but he felt great that he did his best and did not cheat. Unlike the other students, Johnny, Raymond, Charlie, and Curtis left the history class smiling and laughing.

In history class the next day, many of the students were happily surprised that they did much better than they thought on the test. Timothy did very well, and he received an A.

The biggest surprise, however, was the look on Johnny, Raymond, Charlie, and Curtis's faces. They were unaware that Mrs. Washington had decided to make some changes to the test the night before, and they all failed the test!

Mrs. Washington thought it was strange and suspicious that they all had the exact same answers. When she confronted them, they confessed what they had done. Because of their actions, they received detention after school the next week.

The following week during PE class, Timothy and his classmates were excited to play basketball. Coach Tyler, their gym teacher, would always plan for the class to play basketball as the activity on Thursdays. For this Thursday, Coach Tyler announced that the winning team would receive special medals and a victory cake.

"We have to win the medals and the cake," said Johnny.

"Right," agreed Raymond, Charlie, and Curtis.

They knew Coach Tyler always allowed them to choose their teams, so they came up with a plan to make sure they would win. Roy, a kid in their class, had gotten hurt last week and was not able to participate. Coach Tyler had him keep score for the games.

Johnny, Raymond, Charlie, and Curtis convinced Roy to give them three points instead of two for every other basket to help make sure they won the game. They then let Timothy know about their plan.

LUKE 8:17
PROVERBS 10:9
PROVERBS 11:3

As the time to start the game approached, Timothy became more and more unsettled thinking about the plan to cheat in the basketball game. He thought back again to the verses he had learned the last time he visited his grandma's church.

When the time came to pick teams for the basketball game, Johnny, Raymond, Charlie, and Curtis made sure they were on the same team. They all looked at Timothy with a strange expression on their faces when he let them know he had decided to be on the other team.

With about five minutes left to go in the basketball game, Johnny, Raymond, Charlie, and Curtis's team was comfortably ahead on the scoreboard. Roy had given them three points instead of two for every other basket, and Coach Tyler had not noticed.

"Those medals and cake are as good as ours," said Johnny as he fist-bumped Raymond, Charlie, and Curtis.

Despite the confidence they all shared, they were unaware that Principal Adams had been watching the game and the scoreboard at the back of the gym for the last ten minutes.

Immediately after the game, Principal Adams approached Roy about the scoreboard, and he confessed what he did and how he was convinced to do it by Johnny, Raymond, Charlie, and Curtis.

Therefore, the medals and cake were awarded to Timothy's team after Coach Tyler found out what happened. Johnny, Raymond, Charlie, and Curtis had to serve a few more weeks in detention too.

Later that evening, Timothy called his grandma to tell her about his first few weeks at his new school. He told her about many things, but especially about how he earned an A on his history test and how much he loved getting his medal and the victory cake for the basketball game. He also told her how much the verses he had learned at church had helped him.

Grandma Lois said, "I'm very proud of you, Timothy! Remember that God's Word will always help you in times of need, trouble, and in making tough decisions."

Timothy smiled in agreement. He was excited, thinking about the next time he would go to his grandma's church and about the new Scriptures he would learn.

About the Authors

The Bryants are a Christian family who strongly believe in the power of God's Word. They are excited to share this message through *Trusting Timothy: A Story about Cheating*.

To learn more about the Bryants and their next writing adventure, visit trustingtimothy.com or contact them at bryantfamily@trustingtimothy.com.